The Brain on
Quartz Mountain

The Brain on Quartz Mountain

by Margaret J. Anderson

Illustrated by Charles Robinson

ALFRED A. KNOPF

NEW YORK

GRATEFUL ACKNOWLEDGMENT is made to Sterling Publishing Co., Inc. for permission to reprint a portion of *Guinness Book of World Records*. Copyright © 1981 by Sterling Publishing Co., Inc. Published by permission of the copyright owner.

This is a Borzoi Book
Published by Alfred A. Knopf, Inc.

1   3   5   7   9   0   8   6   4   2

Library of Congress Cataloging in Publication Data
Anderson, Margaret Jean, 1931–
The Brain on Quartz Mountain.
(Capers) Summary: Dave's role in Professor Botti's experiment on a chicken's brain helps him compete for a trip to the World Series.
[1. Science—Experiments—Fiction.   2. Baseball—Fiction]   I. Robinson, Charles, 1931–   ill.
II. Title.   III. Series
PZ7.A54397Br 1982   [Fic]   81-23658
ISBN 0-394-95385-1 (lib. bdg.)   AACR2
ISBN 0-394-85385-7 (pbk.)

FOR RICHARD

Contents

The Brain on
Quartz Mountain

1
The Ghost Laboratory

———

THE MOMENT I opened the front door that afternoon I noticed that the house was different. Maybe I just missed the sound of the television. All that winter and spring when I came home from school, Dad had been slumped in an easy chair in front of the TV.

"Paper here yet, Dave?" he would ask.

Then, if the paper had come, he immediately turned to the "Help Wanted" column. It never took long to go through the list of jobs. There wasn't much work in Woodgrove since the lumber mill closed down.

That Friday, however, the sounds in the house were different. Mom was rattling pots and pans. Dad was whistling.

"What's going on?" I asked, looking at all the cardboard boxes piled up in the living room.

Mom came through from the kitchen, pushing her hair back from her forehead. Dad came out of the back room at the same time.

"Tell him, Jim!" Mom said. Her eyes were bright, and she looked younger somehow.

4

"I've got a job, Dave! We're going up to Quartz Mountain Research Station for the summer. I'm going to be caretaker there. Where's the letter about it, Molly?"

It took Mom a while to find the letter in the jumble of papers on the table. It was written on official-looking paper from Cascade University. It said:

Dear Mr. Matheson,

We are pleased to inform you that you have been chosen as caretaker for Quartz Mountain Research Station this summer. Because of budget cuts, the laboratory will not be fully used, but we do expect some scientists to be there by June 1.

You and your family will stay in one of the staff houses. Dr. Barlow will be writing to you with more details about the job.

Yours sincerely,
Jeremy Johnson

"You'll need to get out of school early," Mom said.

"You mean we're going to live up

there?'' I asked, handing the letter back to Dad.

"Yes," Mom said, smiling. "It'll be like having a summer vacation."

Quartz Mountain wasn't the place I'd have chosen for a summer vacation.

"What about baseball?" I asked.

"You'll be able to play baseball up there," Dad answered. "The scientists who work there during the summer bring their families. And there will be college students too."

"But I was going to play for the Woodgrove Little Loggers."

"There's next year," Dad said.

He was wrong about that! This was the last year I could play for the eleven-and-unders. By next year, I'd be twelve, and back to being the youngest on the team with people like Pete Jacob and Marvin Copes hitting home runs and being big heroes. They were in my grade, but both had already turned twelve, and so they couldn't play for the Little Loggers this summer.

That next week I was kept so busy I hardly had time to think about baseball. There were supplies to check, crates to pack, and errands to run. Often my efforts went unappreciated—like the time I nailed a crate shut before it was full. Dad did admit, grudgingly, that I had done a good job of making it secure.

By the last week of May, everything was ready. I sat squeezed into the front seat of the truck between Mom and Dad. We took the north road out of town, winding up beside Obsidian Creek. We passed my favorite fishing place and the swimming hole and then got beyond the stretch of creek I knew.

The road became narrower, steeper. Dad changed gears. I could feel Mom sitting stiffly beside me. She pressed her foot against the floorboard as if she were putting on the brakes, even though we were going uphill. The road wound higher. Now and again, we could see Obsidian Creek way below us in the canyon, its water brown and angry, still swollen with the runoff from melting snow.

I was sure we'd come more than thirty miles. I wanted to ask Dad if we were on the right road, but there was no point. This was the only road.

The trees were smaller up here, with some open meadow, bright with Indian paintbrush and lupins. Then we saw a weathered wooden sign—*Quartz Mountain Research Station, Cascade University*. Beyond the sign were the buildings.

The minute I saw them I felt let down.

Laboratories and research and scientists all sound important and dignified, but these buildings had a temporary look. They were small and untidy compared to the size of the mountains, the forest, and the sky.

The laboratory itself was a square building with a tall cooling tower rising up behind. To the left was the students' dormitory, long and low, with the windows boarded up. On the other side, at right angles to the lab, were the staff houses. They looked like a row of shabby motel units.

"We'll take the one closest to the lab," Dad said, bringing the truck to a quick stop in front of the door.

The rooms smelled musty after being closed so long. Mice and chipmunks had found their way in, in spite of locked doors and boarded windows. I chose the front bedroom. Mom and Dad took the back room. Both bedrooms opened into a combined kitchen and living room that ran the length of the side of the house.

"There's no electricity!" I said, flicking the light switch off and on.

"I have to check the fuses and pull the main switch," Dad said. "It's behind the lab. Do you want to come with me, Dave?"

It would beat helping Mom carry groceries and suitcases in from the truck. I followed Dad eagerly. He suggested that I could make myself useful by taking down the shutters from the lab windows.

When I had finished, Dad unlocked the door. The building seemed bigger inside. First we went down a flight of stone steps to the basement. It was like going into a cave. The dingy cement walls were damp. Pipes and gutters and sinks were all made of gray metal. The bare light bulbs overhead didn't give enough light to reach all the corners.

Upstairs it was more like a real laboratory. The offices had steel cabinets and desks. The biology lab had balances and microscopes. In the chemistry lab dust lay thick on shelves of beakers, jars of chemicals, flasks, and coiled glass tubing. A heavy door was marked with red danger signs. Dad explained that the room beyond that door was strictly off-limits, because they used radioactive materials in there.

"Don't you think it's weird—all this stuff and nobody using it?" I whispered.

Dad agreed. "I've been in a ghost town before, but never a ghost laboratory! It'll be better when a few people get here."

I looked around at the dust, the faded ink on the labels, and a pair of cracked boots laced with cobwebs. I wondered uneasily what sort of experiments scientists would do in a creepy place like this.

2
The Scientists

IT WAS close to supper time on the fifth day when the first scientist arrived. A jeep came roaring up the hill. We all ran out to meet it, as if we were waiting to be rescued from a desert island. The jeep was crammed with all sorts of things. Everything from butterfly nets to a baby's crib.

A tall, lean, bearded man unfolded himself from the front seat. "So this is Quartz Mountain," he said, stretching. Then he shook hands with Dad. "I'm Roy Brown. You must be Jim Matheson. Come on, Betty! Let little Cricket take a look at his new home!"

Little Cricket turned out to be a baby around a year old. Betty pulled him out from among the bundles and set him down on the ground. His face was very red, and his curly blond hair was damp with sweat. He stood swaying for a minute or two, blinking up at us. Then he let us know what he thought about his new home. He opened his mouth and howled.

The Browns decided they would move into the house next door to ours. Dad and I exchanged glances. If the baby was

QUARTZ MOUNTAIN
RESEARCH STATION
CASCADE UNIVERSITY

going to cry like that, we'd sooner they
lived at the other end of the row. But Dad
offered to help them unload. I ended up
carrying in boxes and unpacking them.

I couldn't imagine why the Browns
needed so many books just for one summer. I had brought only one—my *Guinness Book of World Records*. It's my fa-

vorite book. I like it because you can start anywhere, and it's always interesting. I have noticed that a lot of books are really dull at the beginning, but if you skip all the boring parts, it gets confusing.

After the jeep was unloaded, Dad took Roy over to see the lab. Mom held the baby to give Betty a chance to make supper and get settled. She seemed to have forgotten that Dad and I needed to eat too.

I finally went home and opened a can of stew. I was beginning to feel annoyed with this baby for disrupting everything. But mostly I was annoyed because he was too young to play baseball.

When Mom came home, she knew all about the Browns. The baby's real name was Joey, but Roy was studying to be an entomologist. ("Someone who chases bugs," Mom explained, although I already knew that.) That's why Roy gave Joey nicknames like Cricket. Roy wanted to find out about the kinds of insects that lived in the beaver pond. I wondered why anyone—except maybe the beaver—cared.

Later in the evening, when Joey was asleep, I saw Roy and Betty sitting on their front steps. It seemed like a good time to sound them out about organizing a baseball team when more people came, so I wandered over. Right away, I could tell they weren't interested.

"Too competitive," Roy said, shaking his head. "Games should foster friendship. Where's the hacky-sack, Betty?"

Betty stood up. She produced a small,

soft, leather ball from her jeans pocket. It looked like something Joey had been chewing on. She kicked it over to Roy.

"You use the side of your foot, like this," Roy said to me, kicking the hacky-sack to Betty.

They were pretty good, really, the way they could keep it in the air. Almost like juggling. Sometimes Roy passed it from foot to foot, and even headed it, before sending it back to Betty. When I had a chance to kick it, I almost sent it through the window.

"How do we score?" I asked.

Roy shook his head at me, smiling. "No scoring, no rules!" He kicked it back to me.

"Nice going, Dave!" Betty said, encouraging me, when I finally sent it in her direction.

After I improved a bit, we had fun playing hacky-sack. But it wasn't baseball! And I couldn't see Pete Jacob or Marv Copes getting excited about it.

THE NEXT scientist to come was Dr. Hendrix. He had been at the lab last summer, and for several summers before that. He was working on a forestry project. You'd think that if a man was working on something that takes as long to grow as a tree, he would be slow and quiet and patient. But Dr. Hendrix wasn't like that at all. He was jumpy and irritable and very unfriendly.

One morning, just after Dr. Hendrix came, Dad suggested I should make myself useful. I took the lawnmower from the storage shed and cut the patch of grass and weeds out in front of the lab, and down the side of the houses. It improved the place so much that I dragged the mower around to the area behind the lab where the weeds were really tall. Maybe I could cut enough for a baseball diamond.

It was tougher than I expected, and the mower kept jumping about on the rough ground. I was just taking a second run at it when Dr. Hendrix came out of the lab, yelling and waving his arms. I meant to shut the mower off, but I turned the lever the wrong way. The mower went faster, dragging me with it.

"My trees! My trees!" Dr. Hendrix was shouting, still waving his arms. "You're cutting down my trees!"

He didn't need to shout because I had

now shut the mower off. Besides, I was fifty yards from the trees. But then I looked down and saw that he was right. There were some little fir trees growing among the weeds and long grass.

I said I was sorry. After that I tried to avoid Dr. Hendrix. Anyway, he was too old and fat for baseball.

THE THIRD scientist to come was Professor Botti. When he arrived, I didn't realize he had anything to do with the lab at all. That was because of the chickens.

It was a warm afternoon, and I was lying around wishing something would happen. When I heard a car coming, I was out of the house at once. An old Ford rattled into view. It bumped to a standstill, and an old man with a fringe of white hair around his shiny bald head called to me, "Where will I put the chickens?"

"Bring them in here," I answered, opening our front door and showing him the counter by the sink. Mom must have ordered them from Woodgrove. I'd heard her complaining that she was tired of canned meat.

Mom and Betty had taken the baby over to the beaver pond where Roy was collecting insects. It struck me that this chicken man might want to be paid, so I ran off to get Dad. It took me a while to find him. He was lying on his back, tinkering with something under the truck.

"The chicken man's here," I said.

"That'll be Botti," he answered.

"I told him to put the chickens in the kitchen," I said.

"You what?" Dad came out from under the truck so quickly that he bumped his head. It didn't improve his temper. "Where did you say to put the chickens?" He sounded really irritated.

"In the kitchen, Dad."

Dad went striding across the grass. I had to run to keep up. When we got to our house, I understood why Dad was upset. They were live chickens—four hens and a rooster—and Professor Botti had let them loose in our house. Dad stood there, shaking his head in disbelief. He tried to speak, but his voice was drowned out by the rooster. It was perched on the back of one our chairs.

Professor Botti popped out of his car

again, round and red and smiling. He looked like an Irish leprechaun.

"That's a good place for them," he said. "Maybe we could make them a run."

"There's been a mistake!" Dad answered.

"You didn't get my letter?" Professor Botti sounded puzzled.

"I got your letter before we left Woodgrove, Professor," Dad said, a little sharply. "I was expecting you *and* the chickens. I've built a run for them. It's just that you happen to have let them loose in my home."

"But the boy said—"

"Never mind what the boy said! We've got to get these chickens out of the house."

It was only after we'd caught the chickens that Dad suddenly thought it all very funny. He told me to put the house to rights, and went off to show the professor the real chicken house, roaring with laughter. But I wasn't laughing. One of those mean chickens had pecked the back of my hand. And Dad had left me to clean up the mess. How was I to know they were live chickens? Why blame me? Why not blame the crazy professor?

3
Woodgrove Again

Two GEOLOGISTS, Hank and Steve, made their headquarters at the lab. I think they were hoping for another Mount St. Helens. They had a lot of equipment for measuring earth tremors which they were setting up all through the Cascade Mountains. It must have been very sensitive equipment. It measured the earth shaking when I jumped near it. Since that was the only tremor they recorded all summer, they should have been more pleased.

Then some men from the Forest Service moved in for a few days and fixed up phone lines. We were to call in a report if we saw a forest fire starting anywhere. For the first few days after the phones were put in, I went about straining my eyes for columns of smoke. By that time I was so bushed that it would have been exciting to talk on a phone. I thought about calling Pete or Marv down in Woodgrove, but what was there to say? I didn't want to hear how their baseball team was doing.

A class of college students and their teacher overran the lab for a week. They treated us permanent residents as if we were an obscure tribe of aborigines. They probably went home with notes in their loose-leaf notebooks headed "native sub-species."

Other scientists came and stayed for a few days or a few weeks. They seemed to spend all their time working and talking. No one suggested baseball.

The only person who never joined in the discussions was Professor Botti. He lived by himself in the house at the far end of the row. Each morning, he passed our house on his way to feed his chickens.

"I wish he'd give us some fresh eggs," Mom said, seeing him pass the window.

"They're for his experiments," Dad answered.

I wondered what sort of experiments he did with an egg.

The next morning, I followed him. He picked up three eggs and headed straight over to the lab. So he wasn't going to have them for breakfast!

Professor Botti worked in the chemistry lab. I had noticed that he always kept the door closed. I gave him time to get inside. Then I carefully boosted myself up to the window and peered in. I was just in time to see the professor disappear through the heavy door with the warning sign on it. He was still carrying the eggs.

I pressed closer to the window to get a better view of the lab. It was like a scene from a movie—a mad scientist movie. Chemicals bubbled in flasks connected to each other by coiled glass tubing. Beakers and jars were everywhere. Some-

DANGER

RADIOACTIVE
- MATERIALS

thing that looked like salt glowed strangely in the pan of a balance.

The heavy door swung open. Professor Botti came back into the lab, still carrying the three eggs. I dropped out of sight. I didn't want him to see me.

THE NEXT DAY, Roy asked if I'd like to go down to Woodgrove with him to pick up supplies. When we got into town, I was surprised at the number of people and the noise of the cars. I said to Roy that Woodgrove had never been this busy before.

As we were carrying the last load of groceries out of the Dollar-Valu Market to the jeep, Pete and Marv were crossing the parking lot. I yelled to them. I'd been hoping we would run into them.

"I thought you were up at Quartz Mountain," Pete said.

"We're just down to buy groceries," I answered.

"Can you come over to the park and play ball?" Pete asked. He was cradling a new baseball in his mitt.

There was nothing I would have liked better, but Roy was waiting in the jeep.

"I have to go," I said.

"Let's see if we can find Bill," Marv said, moving away.

"Do you play ball at Quartz Mountain?" Pete asked. "They had a team up there one year. It came down to play in Woodgrove."

"We don't have time for ballgames," I answered loftily. "The scientists are all too busy with their experiments."

"What sort of experiments?" Pete asked.

"Top-secret stuff," I said. "I'm not allowed to talk about it."

"Come on, Pete," Marv said impatiently.

Pete began to follow him.

Top secret! Chicken eggs and bugs and trees! What had made me say that?

"Is that a new ball, Pete?" I asked quickly. I wanted to talk for a few minutes longer. Roy could wait.

"I won it," Pete said proudly. "On a quiz show on the radio."

" 'Brain Scan'?" I asked.

Pete nodded. "Three-time winners get a chance to be on TV in Salem."

"I wish I could try," I said, looking enviously at Pete's white ball.

"There's nothing to stop you," Pete said. "You phone in the answers."

Roy gave a short toot on the horn, so I had to go. But Pete had given me something to think about. If *he* could win a baseball, then I bet I could too. "Brain

Scan" was a quiz show on our local radio station, and the questions were pretty easy. It was just a case of being the first one to call in.

And if I had a new ball like Pete's, then surely someone would want to play baseball up on Quartz Mountain.

4
The Mad Scientist

——

MOM WAS kneading bread dough in the kitchen.

"Where's my radio, Mom?" I asked. I wanted to listen to "Brain Scan" at ten o'clock.

"I loaned it to Professor Botti," Mom said.

"To Professor Botti?" I asked in surprise. "Why?"

"He doesn't have one, and he wanted to listen to it. I suppose."

"But there's a program *I* want to hear," I wailed.

"Then ask to borrow it back."

"He'd be in his lab just now," I argued. "You said I wasn't to bother people when they were working."

"I expect it would be all right this once," Mom said. "And it's only Professor Botti."

"What do you mean—*only* Professor Botti?" I asked.

Mom looked flustered. "Roy and Betty say he's a bit crazy. All that science—and working on his own so much." Mom pounded the dough some more, then continued, "He retired several years ago, but still keeps on with his research. The university lets him use the lab up here in the summers."

"What does he do?" I asked.

"Nobody really knows," Mom answered. "Roy says they never will. The professor never tells anyone about his experiments, and never writes papers about them."

"So I should just go over and ask for the radio?" I asked, with an eye on the clock.

"Remember to be polite!" Mom called after me as I left.

I KNOCKED on the chemistry lab door, but no one answered. I pushed it open and walked in. Professor Botti, wearing a stained lab coat, was perched on a high stool by a bench. He was peering down a microscope. Occasionally he made quick notes in a small, black notebook. His face glowed in the bluish light of a Bunsen burner. In the far corner, my radio and a small portable television set were both turned on, though no one was listening to them.

I cleared my throat several times before the professor looked up. I didn't miss the anxious look that flickered across his eyes. "What do you want, boy?" he asked sharply.

"I came to get my radio," I said.

"I'm using it."

That wasn't true. It was across the room, and turned down so low that he could hardly hear it. But I remembered Mom saying to be polite, and so I asked if

I could borrow it for half an hour.

"Can you read?" he asked.

"Of course," I answered.

"Then maybe we can strike a bargain."

It didn't seem fair to have to bargain to borrow the radio. After all, it was mine. But there was something so weird about the professor and his lab that I asked, "What kind of bargain, sir?"

"First, I have to tell you about my experiments," Professor Botti said in a low voice. He got up and looked out into the hallway. He closed the door. Then he checked the windows.

By this time, I expected to hear something really exciting. But it was quite dull, and a bit confusing. Later, I looked up some of the words the professor had used in the books Roy had brought with him. And I asked Roy questions. But carefully, because Profesor Botti had sworn me to secrecy. Gradually, the professor's work began to make sense—in a senseless sort of way.

Professor Botti was a geneticist—a scientist who studies how characteristics are passed from parents to children. Like blue-eyed parents have blue-eyed children, but brown-eyed parents can have either blue- or brown-eyed children. It depends on the genes. Occasionally, a gene can change. That's called a *mutation*. (I found that word in Roy's books.) Professor Botti was also an embryologist. That's someone who studies how animals grow, from the very beginning, even before they are born. Or in the professor's case, before they are hatched, because he experimented with chickens.

In the beginning, there is a single cell. It divides, and divides again—and again, and again, and again. With chickens, some of these cells eventually become a wing, some a leg, some the heart, and so on. When the cells reached a certain stage, Professor Botti took a few of them—a *culture* he called it—and grew them in a salt solution in a test tube.

He pointed to rows of jars and beakers on the shelf above his head. I peered up at them, expecting to see wings and legs and breasts, like cut-up chicken in packages in the supermarket. But the liquid in the jars was cloudy, so I couldn't really see anything.

"Are you going to put them back together again?" I asked. Sometimes when I doodle I draw birds with four legs or two heads. I imagined Professor Botti doing this for real.

He shook his head. "I'm finding out about changes in the genes," he said. "If I work with parts of the animal, I get results faster. And the results are easier to understand. I'm interested on the effects of radiation on a cell."

So that was why he had taken the chicken eggs through the door with the warning signs.

A strange, secretive look crossed Professor Botti's face. He led me over to the corner where my radio was playing. He pointed to a jar with a shapeless gray mass in it.

"What do you think that is?" he asked.

I shook my head. I had no idea. Then, suddenly, I did know! It was almost as if the thing in the jar had whispered the answer.

"A brain," I said. "A chicken brain."

Professor Botti nodded, smiling. "These are brain cells."

"But no chicken ever had a brain that big," I said. Even through the cloudy liquid in the jar I could see that the brain was almost as big as my closed fist.

"I've been feeding it," the professor explained. "That's the wonderful thing about growing things in jars. They can keep right on growing. When this jar gets too small, I'll put it in a bigger one."

"What are you going to do with it?" I asked uneasily.

It made me feel nervous, though I wasn't sure why. After all, it couldn't move.

"I'm teaching it," Professor Botti answered solemnly. "It already knows the basics of mathematics and language."

"You mean it can talk?" I asked.

"Not exactly," Professor Botti said. "It tells me things by telepathy. It thinks things from its brain into my brain. Though not everyone can receive its messages."

I remembered how I had known right off that it was a brain. Maybe it had told me.

"Why are you teaching it?" I asked.

"It will be like having a live computer," the professor answered. "I fill the brain cells with facts. Then when I need them, I ask it a question and it passes the answer back to my brain."

"How much does it know?"

"It has been learning from the radio and television. The only problem is, that

49

to be of any use, it has to go far beyond anything it can learn from TV. I want it to know chemistry and physics and astronomy. That's where you can help."

"Me?" I squeaked. "I don't know chemistry or physics or stuff like that!"

"You can read," the old man pointed out.

I nodded

"All you need to do is to read to it," Professor Botti explained. "The Brain will do the rest."

So that is how I began to teach the Brain.

5
The Brain

___

IT WAS sometimes hard to find time to read to the Brain. Mom needed help hanging out the washing. Betty wanted me to mind Cricket while she did some sewing. Dad said the grass needed cutting. Roy asked me to go with him in the jeep to a beaver pond on the other side of the mountain to see if the bugs were dif-

ferent there. Even Dr. Hendrix asked me to help him collect fir cones. I was the most popular person at the entire research station.

But I did manage to read every day. It was weird sitting there in the corner of the lab reading to a canning jar. And every day, the Brain and I tuned in to "Brain Scan." Professor Botti had a phone in the lab, but so far I hadn't needed to use it. I never knew the answers to the questions. I began to think that Pete's older brother must have helped him win the ball.

The chemistry book I was given to read was really dull with long words I couldn't pronounce. I half expected the Brain to scold me for not reading properly. Sometimes I was tempted to skip bits, but that might mix the Brain up. Besides, the book was just as boring farther on.

The book on astronomy wasn't quite so bad. It started out with things I knew, like the names of planets. I read them over slowly: Mercury, Venus, Earth, Mars, Jupiter, Saturn, Uranus, Neptune, Pluto. There was a table with interesting facts about the planets, and I read that twice because the Brain wanted me to.

It's hard to say how I knew this, but sometimes I could feel the Brain responding. I had the idea that it liked me.

The next morning, the subject on "Brain Scan" was astronomy. I was so excited that I began to dial the station number before Ted, the announcer, had finished asking the question.

The quiz show worked like this: The first person to call in with the correct answer was then asked another question on the same subject. Usually a harder question. To win the baseball, both answers had to be right.

Ted's voice was asking over the radio, "What planet is closest to the sun?"

The phone was already ringing.

"We have an eager caller on that question," Ted continued.

I turned the radio down.

"Your answer is . . . ?"

"Mercury," I said.

"Right on! And your name is . . . ?"

"Dave Matheson," I answered. My voice sounded queer.

"Do you live here in Woodgrove, Dave?" Ted asked.

"Yes . . . no!" I was getting confused. "I'm living up on Quartz Mountain for the summer."

"Practically in outer space yourself!" Ted laughed. "And now, for a brand new baseball, can you tell me how long a year is on Mercury?"

I had forgotten there would be another question. My mind went blank. I stared at the canning jar as the seconds ticked silently away. The answer was in that table I had been reading to the Brain. Then I felt the Brain sending me a message.

"A year on Mercury is eighty-eight days," I said.

"Well done, Dave!" Ted's voice boomed in my ear. "Next time you're in the big city, drop by and we'll give you your baseball."

"Thank you! Thank you, sir!" I said. But Ted was already introducing a commercial. "And thank *you!*" I added, talking to the Brain.

I WENT on reading to the Brain. I felt that now we were really friends. One day it told me quite clearly that these books of Professor Botti's were boring. It didn't want to listen to them anymore. So the next day I brought my *Guinness Book of World Records.*

"Today, you're going to learn something entirely new," I said solemnly to the canning jar. I felt a stirring of interest. "I'm going to read to you about baseball."

Professor Botti was, as usual, peering down his microscope on the other side of the room. He took no more notice of me than he had of the radio or TV.

I opened my book to the section on sports. I cleared my throat, and read:

"*Origins.* The Reverend Thomas Wilson, of Maidstone, Kent, England, wrote disapprovingly, in 1700, of baseball being played on Sundays. It is also referred to in *Northanger Abbey* by Jane Austen, c. 1798.

"*Home Runs.* Henry L. ("Hank") Aaron broke the major league record set by George H. ("Babe") Ruth of 714 home runs in a lifetime when he hit number 715 on April 8, 1974."

The Brain was so interested in baseball that I read the entire section through twice and then went on to basketball, billiards, bobsledding, and bowling.

The Brain wasn't interested only in

sports. It also liked to hear about animals, photography, weather, music, and numbers. I read the chapters on "The Universe and Space" and "The Scientific World" very carefully because Professor Botti wanted the Brain to learn science.

Although the *Guinness Book of World Records* was easier to read than the chemistry book, it did have hard words in it. Especially in the section on longest words. The longest word in *Webster's Dictionary* has forty-five letters. And there's a man whose last name has five hundred and ninety letters. I didn't try to read that.

We still listened to "Brain Scan" each morning. One day the question came right out of the *Guinness Book of World Records*. When I heard Ted asking,

"Who broke Babe Ruth's home run record?" I set a new record in the speed of dialing a phone number.

"Hank Aaron," I answered breathlessly.

"What was the number of the home run that broke the record?"

I looked steadily at the Brain and waited for it to give me the answer. "Henry L. ("Hank") Aaron broke the major league record set by George H. ("Babe") Ruth of 714 home runs in a lifetime when he hit Number 715 on April 8, 1974." The Brain told me this as clearly as if I was reading it from the book.

"Aaron's seven hundred and fifteenth run broke the record," I said.

"Very good! Very good!" Ted sang out. "And what's your name?"

"Dave Matheson," I answered.

"Dave Matheson!" Ted said. "The brain on Quartz Mountain!"

I nearly dropped the phone. How did he know?

It turned out that he was only joking with me. He went on to say that I had now won a baseball mitt. One more correct answer and I'd qualify to appear on the television version of the game in Salem.

"Keep trying, Dave! Good luck!"

6
The Dream

I WAS now more eager than ever to teach the Brain. I borrowed books from Roy and Betty. I even started to read the dictionary, but I gave up before I was through the A's. We tuned in to all the TV game shows, and I read from the *Book of World Records* during commercials.

Sometimes Professor Botti came over

and talked to the Brain. I was worried that he would find out I'd been teaching it the wrong things, but he always seemed satisfied with the answers the Brain gave him.

The professor was working on a new feeding solution for his cultures. It looked like plain water, but Professor Botti said that tap water would kill the brain cells. This was more like sea water with some extra chemicals in it. He tried some out on the Brain. The Brain began to grow—fast. It grew so much that we had to put it in a quart canning jar instead of a pint jar.

I was happy about this. I needed its help if I was going to win again on "Brain Scan." Twice recently, I had known the answer, but someone else had dialed the number ahead of me. What we needed was the answer to a hard question that no one else knew. I worried that the summer would be over before I had another chance to call in.

To make matters worse, Roy kept asking me to help him with his bugs. I think Mom put him up to it because she thought I spent too much time in Professor Botti's lab. So I often had to go to the beaver pond for the afternoon or evening.

I wished that the Brain could come along too. It was very educational being with Roy. He talked all the time, mostly about bugs. Some days the Brain could have learned more from listening to Roy than from me reading all those books.

Until Roy told me, I didn't know that young dragonflies live underwater. He showed me water beetles that have an aqualung. And caddisflies that spin fishing nets. And tiny shrimps with lots of legs.

Roy's main interest was dragonflies. Sometimes we chased the adults with a net. I was horrified when he put a beautiful big green one in his killing bottle.

"I don't see how you can go around killing things," I said angrily. "After all, you're a vegetarian!"

"I'm not going to eat it!" Roy laughed.

"I thought it was *killing,* not *eating,* that you are against," I said. It felt good to win an argument.

Roy said nothing.

A few minutes later, when I slapped a mosquito, he asked me why a dragonfly had more right to live than a mosquito.

"Mosquitoes bite," I said.

"Can't you spare one drop of blood so that a poor mother mosquito can nourish her children?" Roy asked. "You can have your right to life for dragonflies, but I want equal rights for mosquitoes!"

The trouble was I could never tell when Roy was teasing.

SOMETIMES Joey came with us, and then there was no time for talking. Joey would have eaten a dragonfly if he'd caught one! He was forever popping things into his mouth.

One of his favorite games was throwing stones into the water. One afternoon I collected a great pile of stones for him to throw into the shallow water. I only turned my back for a minute and there he was throwing Roy's collecting jars into the pond instead of the stones. It was easier to read to the Brain than to mind Joey.

That evening Mom told me that she and Betty were planning to go to Woodgrove for groceries the next day. "Betty wonders if you could babysit Joey for an hour or two in the morning," Mom said. "Just while Roy does his collecting. Then

Roy can give Joey lunch, and mind him in the afternoon."

"I have to listen to 'Brain Scan' in the morning," I said.

"Bring the radio over here," Mom answered. "Why don't you go and get it now?"

"Professor Botti likes me to come to the lab in the mornings," I said.

"Surely he can manage without you for once," Mom said sharply.

When I was picking up the radio, I suddenly got the idea of taking the Brain home too. Professor Botti would never miss it. And if he did, I would tell him I'd been reading to it. I could read to it while I was babysitting Cricket.

I smuggled the Brain into my bedroom and set it on the table near my bed. It seemed to be excited to be outside the lab at last. I could feel its curiosity.

THAT NIGHT was the first time I had the nightmare about the Brain.

I dreamed that it was growing bigger. So big that it poured out of the jar like a giant jellyfish. It flowed over the table and oozed onto my pillow. I jerked away so fast that I woke myself up. I lay still with my heart pounding, afraid to turn on the light to find out if the jar was empty or not. The window was open. The thin curtains were blowing with the same rippling movement as the Brain in my dream.

I finally forced myself to reach out and switch on the light. The Brain was still in its jar. But I was sure it had grown bigger. And the messages reaching my brain weren't friendly. The Brain was angry, as if it blamed me for keeping it imprisoned. I decided to leave the light on.

I only slept off and on for the rest of the night. And when I did sleep, I dreamed about the Brain again. Sometimes it was after me. Sometimes it was after Joey, and that seemed worse.

It was a relief when morning came.

When Betty brought Cricket over for me to babysit, I could see that she was upset.

"I don't know if I should go, Molly," she said to my Mom. "Joey didn't sleep well last night. He kept waking up crying, almost as if he was having bad dreams."

Joey had just been bathed. He was all pink and freshly scrubbed.

"He looks fine now," Mom said. I knew she was really looking forward to her day in town. She wanted Betty to go too, because Betty was going to drive. Mom didn't care for mountain roads, but Betty liked driving the jeep.

"He'll be okay," I promised. Joey couldn't feel much worse than I did.

"Maybe he'll have a nap this morning," Betty said. "But you will watch him carefully, won't you, Dave? He can climb out of his crib now."

After Mom and Betty left, I gave Joey some toys to keep him happy, and I began to read to the Brain. Even though I was reading from the Brain's favorite book, the *Guinness Book of World*

Records, it didn't listen. It was interested only in Joey. It's hard to say how I knew this. Maybe by the way Joey acted. He didn't bang his toys around the way he usually did. He just sat staring at the canning jar as if he was hypnotized.

It was time for "Brain Scan." I tried to get the Brain's attention so that it would help me with the answers.

Ted was already asking the first question. "Name an animal with two legs, one with four legs, six legs, eight legs, and ten legs."

I knew that without any help from the Brain! I dialed the number. The phone was ringing.

"A man, a dog, a beetle, a spider, and a crab," I said breathlessly.

"Now name an animal that has only one foot," Ted said.

I didn't even need to think. Roy had told me that.

"A snail," I said.

I was a three-time winner! I would get to be on TV. After Ted had congratulated me, there was no one to share the excitement with. I grabbed Joey and rushed outside. Who should I see but Dr. Hen-

drix going out to look at his little trees.

"I'm going to be on TV!" I yelled.

When I calmed down enough to tell him all about winning "Brain Scan," he was nearly as excited as I was. He was even impressed that I had already won a baseball and mitt.

"You've got to get that ball and mitt up here so that we can have a baseball game before summer's over," Dr. Hendrix said. "We used to have a team here. I've really missed those baseball games this summer!"

Sometimes you can be quite wrong about people.

7
The Radio Station

A FEW DAYS later I got a letter from the radio station telling me the date I was to be on television in Salem. Just thinking about it made me shake. The letter also asked me to come to the radio station in Woodgrove the following Tuesday. They wanted to give me the baseball and mitt. And they had a few questions to ask me.

"I've answered enough questions," I said when I read the letter.

"They have to be sure you're smart enough to be on TV," Mom said. "After all, someone could have been helping you."

I thought Dad would grumble about having to take me to Woodgrove one week and Salem the next week. But he was really excited about me being on TV. He kept calling me his Whiz Quiz Kid.

I was worried about these questions they were going to ask at the radio station. Was it some kind of test? Without the help of the Brain, I likely couldn't pass. Then I wouldn't be on TV. I hated to think how disappointed Mom and Dad and Roy and Betty would be. Even Hank and Steve, the geologists, were excited.

They had rigged up a taller antenna so that we could get better reception on Professor Botti's small TV set. Everyone was going to watch.

I couldn't let all these people down. I decided the Brain would have to go to Woodgrove with me. I made a handle for the jar out of a piece of string. Then, just before we left, I smuggled the jar out to the back of our truck. The Brain liked this new experience. I could tell that it was excited.

When we reached the radio station, I told Dad I wanted to go in alone.

"Okay, Dave," he said. "I'll meet you back here. Good luck!" He thumped me on the shoulder.

I watched him walk away. Then I got the Brain out of the back of the truck. It had had a rough ride. I hoped it hadn't forgotten anything. I carried it gently into the radio station.

A blond girl, chewing gum, stopped me at the front desk. "Who do you want to see?" she asked.

"I'm Dave Matheson," I said.

She raised her eyebrows and went on chewing her gum.

"I won in 'Brain Scan,' " I told her.

"Ted," she called. "Someone for you."

Ted wasn't a bit like his voice. I had thought he would be young and good-looking, with thick, black hair. Instead, he was quite old, with thin, brown hair combed over his bald patch. He had a long, sharp nose.

I wasn't what he expected either.

"I thought you'd be older," Ted said.

He glanced down at the canning jar. "Been collecting frog spawn?"

I turned red. I set the Brain carefully down on the corner of the desk. I was shaking so much, I was jiggling the liquid out of the jar. The Brain needed a chance to settle down if it was going to help me answer Ted's questions. But I didn't need any help. Ted just asked me my age, my grade in school, and things like that.

Then Ted read over the rules for the TV quiz show. "You have to choose two subject areas," he said. "What do you know most about?"

"Sports," I said quickly.

"What else?"

I couldn't think of anything else.

"How about biology?" Ted asked helpfully, looking at the jar.

I nodded. As soon as I got home I'd start reading Roy's biology book to the Brain.

"I hope you win the grand prize," Ted said. "A trip to the World Series."

"Is that what the prize is?" I asked.

"A trip for two to the World Series," Ted repeated.

Now that was a prize I'd like to win!

When I went out, Dad was waiting for me. He was so interested in my new baseball and mitt that he didn't seem to notice the canning jar that I set carefully between the grocery bags in the back of the truck.

8
The Storm

———

THE BRAIN was growing again. Professor Botti now kept it in a fish bowl.

"I don't like it," Professor Botti muttered, more to himself than to me. "I don't like it at all."

Neither did I! How was I going to smuggle a fish bowl into the TV studio? Even a canning jar would have been difficult.

When I first heard I was going to be on TV, I hadn't planned to take the Brain with me. But then there was such a fuss about me being the Whiz Quiz Kid that I grew scared. I was afraid I'd let everyone down. I imagined them all at home, knowing the answers, while I sat dumb in front of the camera. I didn't have to win the grand prize or anything like that. I just didn't want them to be ashamed of me.

Professor Botti was chewing on a yellow pencil. He was staring at the Brain. "I don't want you to read to it anymore," he said suddenly.

"But I like reading to it," I said. "It's learning biology now, sir."

"No more reading," the professor repeated sternly. "The experiment is over. I'm going to empty out my cultures."

"But, sir . . ." I protested, following the professor across the room.

"There's enough trouble in this world without me adding something that could be used to hurt people," Professor Botti said, reaching for a jar and dumping the contents into the sink. A faintly iodine smell, like seaweed at high-tide mark, began to fill the room.

I looked over at the Brain sitting there quietly thinking over all the things I had read to it. How could it possibly hurt anyone? I couldn't let the professor dump it out along with the chicken wings and legs and breasts. I had to save it. I'd hide it somewhere and leave the fish bowl empty. Maybe I could even put some frog spawn in its place. Meantime I needed a container to put the Brain in for now.

The ideas forming in my mind seemed to come from the Brain itself. I dashed out of the lab, running toward home.

I was only halfway across the grass when I heard a crash. I ran back to the lab. Professor Botti was lying on the floor, his leg bent under him in an awkward position. His overturned stool lay beside him. He must have fallen while trying to reach some jars on the top shelf.

The professor's face was gray, and he was in great pain. But he managed to whisper, "The Brain did it, Dave. The Brain made me fall off the stool. You must get rid of it. Get rid of the Brain. Get rid of all my cultures. The experiment is over. No one must know what I did. It's too dangerous!"

I hardly listened to what he was say-

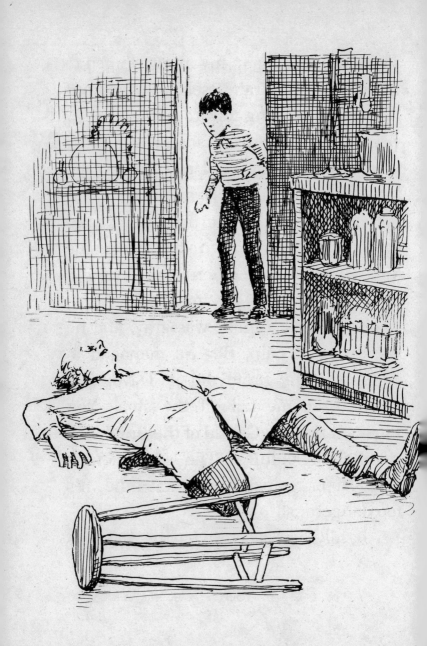

ing. I knew I shouldn't move him. Not without help. Betty had taken a first-aid course. Once again, I dashed out of the lab.

Everyone came running. Betty put a splint on the leg so that the professor could be lifted into Hank's station wagon. Hank and Dad were going to take him to Woodgrove.

"Stand back, Dave," someone said impatiently.

But the professor was still trying to talk to me.

"Promise me, boy!" he said, his eyes fixed on mine. "Say you'll do it!"

"I'll do it," I answered quickly.

The old man relaxed, satisfied.

PROFESSOR BOTTI was taken to the big

hospital in Salem. Even though he hardly ever spoke to anyone, and spent all his time alone in the lab, the research station seemed empty without him. The next day we were all nervous and unsettled. Mom and Dad snapped at each other. Roy had overslept and blamed Betty. Joey threw a tantrum after breakfast. I didn't feel too good either. I had dreamed again about the Brain. It was after Joey.

I went over to the lab to see the Brain. It didn't seem sinister now, the way it did in my dreams. It was glad to see me. I read to it all morning.

Before I went home for lunch, I dumped out all the professor's jars. But I didn't dump out the Brain. When Professor Botti's leg was better, he'd thank me for saving the Brain. Besides, Professor

Botti was wrong not to share the results of his experiments. Roy said that's what science was all about. Sharing knowledge.

But I began to dread bedtime. The dreams were getting worse. I dreamed that the Brain was oozing through the open window. After I closed the window, it seeped under the door. Then it would be after Joey. I would waken to hear him crying in the next house.

At other times, I dreamed about being on TV. This was almost as bad. I could never answer any of the questions. People laughed. Sometimes Roy and Betty. Sometimes Pete and Marv and other kids from school. I woke up sweating.

On the third night after Professor Botti's accident we had a thunderstorm.

Lightning flashed, thunder rolled, the wind howled, and the first heavy drops of rain beat against my window. I burrowed under the covers, trying to shut out the anger of the storm.

Then I heard someone pounding on our door. A hysterical voice was shouting, "Molly! Jim! Wake up! Joey's gone! Has anyone seen Joey?"

Surely this was another nightmare. Joey couldn't really be missing. Not on a night like this.

Dad opened the door, and I heard low, worried voices. I dragged myself out of bed.

Between sobs, Betty was telling her story again, trying to make us understand.

"I went through to check on Joey,"

she said. "He's been waking up a lot lately. His crib was empty. He can climb out of it now. And then I found the front door open."

"Had you locked it before you went to bed?" Dad asked.

Betty shook her head. "We never bother to up here. And the catch isn't very good. It could have blown open in this wind."

"You're sure Joey isn't in the house?" Mom asked.

"We've looked everywhere. Roy's looking outside now. But it's so dark. . . ." Betty's voice trailed off. She began to cry again.

Quite suddenly, I knew what had happened to Joey. The Brain was after him! The Brain wanted to be more than just a

Brain. It wanted to be a person. That's what Professor Botti had meant when he said it might hurt someone. That's why I had been having those dreams. The Brain had been trying to reach me while I slept. And Joey, too. Joey had been sleeping badly ever since the Brain had grown big enough to want to control us. I had been able to fight against it, but Joey was too young to be a match for the Brain.

Without stopping to put on shoes or a jacket, I went tearing across the grass that lay between the house and the lab. The big Douglas fir was whipping back and forth. The sky looked like a stormy sea. I expected to find Joey outside the lab door, but he wasn't there.

I ran around the side of the building. A

sheet of lightning lit up the whole wall like a flash photograph. And in the middle of the picture was Joey. He was straining up toward the open window as if he was being drawn in. His little out-

spread hands were scrabbling at the wall like he was reaching for a grip on the windowsill.

"Joey! Joey!" I called out, throwing my arms around him. He felt stiff, like a big plastic doll, and his eyes were blank and staring. Then he began to cry. I picked him up and ran, stumbling, back over the grass to take him to Betty.

I didn't wait for her to thank me. There was something else I had to do. I grabbed the lab keys from the nail where they hung in the kitchen and ran back to the chemistry lab. I let myself in and crossed to the corner where the fish bowl sat. I picked it up and carried it to the sink. I knew what I was going to do.

Then I stopped. What about the quiz show? It was only two days away. I couldn't answer the questions on my own. I didn't want to look stupid on TV. Not with everyone watching.

But those weren't my thoughts! They were coming from the Brain. The Brain was playing for time.

I concentrated instead on how the Brain had made poor Professor Botti fall. I thought about little Joey. The way he threw stones into the pond and laughed at the splashes. The way he thought he was hiding when he closed his eyes. He had to learn things his own way. And he was pretty smart already!

But I still hesitated, thinking of the good times we'd had. The Brain began quoting some of the interesting things we'd read—the biggest family, the longest ride on a Ferris wheel, and the man with a beard of bees. It reminded me about winning the baseball. But there was also the Brain of my dreams, oozing across my pillow, taking over my mind.

I hurled the whole fish bowl into the sink. It smashed. The smell of iodine and rotting seaweed was strong. The Brain

needed its own salt solution to live in. I turned on both taps and let the water run.

By the time I reached home, Mom had made hot chocolate. We all sat around drinking it. We listened to the sounds of the storm. The thunder was grumbling now, moving farther away.

Joey climbed up on my knee. He snuggled against me, soft and warm, saying, "Da-da-da!"

"Listen to Joey!" I said. "He knows my name!"

"He's a smart kid!" Roy said proudly.

Everyone was laughing and talking. It was like a party. But I was the only one who knew what we were celebrating.

9

The Television
Show

———

THE DAY of the quiz show came all too
soon—for me, anyway. How could I appear on TV when I didn't know anything? I wished I had never met the
crazy professor with that awful experiment of his. To top it all off, Dad still
called me his Whiz Quiz Kid.

"He's just nervous," Mom said to Dad
at breakfast.

"Do you think he'd be happier if I went along with him?" Dad asked. "When Dr. Hendrix said he had to go down to Salem today anyway, and offered to take Dave, it seemed silly not to let him."

"It'll save a lot on gas," Mom agreed.

They were talking as if I wasn't there. I had just told them I felt sick. I said I didn't think I could go.

Roy popped his head around the door and asked, "How's the brain today?"

Then I nearly was sick.

"Don't get stage fright," Betty said, coming in behind him. "I'm going to let Joey stay up to watch you on TV tonight, Dave."

Great! One more person to see me make a fool of myself!

Then Dr. Hendrix came by and said it was time to go. Mom began pulling my collar straight and smoothing my hair as if there were TV cameras waiting outside the door.

Dr. Hendrix was going to a meeting at the university in Salem. We were going to spend the night with some friends of his. I wondered what we'd talk about for two days. But that was nothing compared to worrying about being on TV. If only we could have another thunderstorm. Then maybe the transformer would be struck by lightning.

MY FIRST sight of the TV studio was a bit like my first sight of the lab. I had expected more. The studio was down in the basement of a big building. The set for the quiz show was very small. Just a square of shag carpet, with two walls meeting at an angle behind it. One wall had brickwork painted on it. The other had a picture. The contestants sat on plastic chairs behind a low table with a plant on it. Mom told me later that she thought we were in a big, fancy living room. In fact, there was hardly space to sit.

Beyond the patch of carpet was bare cement. People wheeled in lights and cameras. They tripped over each other, and over the wires and cables that snaked everywhere.

The cameramen kept changing the lights and the focus and the angle. They were more nervous than I was. The other contestants had arrived, and a cameraman ran test pictures on each of us.

There was one woman, Nora, and she was about as old as Mom. Albert was sixteen. The fourth contestant, a stout man named Roger, had been on TV before. He thought he knew so much he wanted to run the whole show. Then there was the announcer, Jon. He made a big deal of me being only eleven.

When the show started, I wasn't a bit nervous. I thought we were just practicing. The questions were pretty easy. It was only when we took a break for a commercial that I found out we had been on the air. I also found out that I was doing really well. A lot of the sports questions were straight out of the *Guinness Book of World Records*. I could answer

the biology questions because I'd read so much to the Brain. I hadn't really thought about how much *I* had learned from those books.

It was too bad we had that commercial. It gave me a chance to see the scores. It also gave me a chance to become nervous.

Roger was in the lead by five points. I came second. Nora and Albert were quite a long way behind.

Jon was explaining the rules for the final question. "This time you pick a category out of a hat," he said. He waved a hat in front of us. "If you think a contestant has given a wrong answer, you can challenge him. Then, if you know the right answer, you collect double the points. But if you challenge a correct answer, the first person scores double, and you lose points."

I had no idea what he was talking about. I decided I'd only answer my own question.

We drew our subjects out of the hat. I looked at mine. *Literature!* That meant books like Shakespeare and *Huckleberry Finn*. Well, even the Brain couldn't have helped me on literature.

Roger was looking smug. He must have got something he knew about.

"Are you ready for your question, Dave?" Jon asked.

I tried to look intelligent. (Later, Betty asked me why I made a face at Jon just then.)

"Name a novel written by Jane Austen."

I stared at Jon. That wasn't a *literature* question. It was a baseball question! Right out of the *Guinness Book of World Records*. The paragraph was as clear in my mind as if the Brain were right there sending it to me.

Origins. The Reverend Thomas Wilson, of Maidstone, Kent, England, wrote disapprovingly, in 1700, of baseball being played on Sundays. It is also referred to in *Northanger Abbey* by Jane Austen, c. 1798.

"Northanger Abbey," I said in a small voice. I sounded a bit uncertain because I wasn't sure how to pronounce it.

"I challenge that!" Roger said in a deep voice.

"Northanger Abbey is an acceptable answer," Jon ruled. "Dave is awarded

ten points. Roger loses five."

Now I was in the lead by ten points. Roger couldn't catch up unless someone challenged his answer. No one did!

After the show, everyone made a huge fuss over me. They all seemed to think I was some kind of genius. Being the Whiz Quiz Kid was pretty wearing. I smiled and nodded a lot.

10
Home Run

———

THE NEXT morning Dr. Hendrix took me to see Professor Botti in the hospital. The nurse wasn't going to let me in, but then she recognized me from TV, and so she made an exception.

The professor looked small and old, propped up against the starched white pillows. "Has everything been taken care of at the lab?'' he whispered anxiously to me.

"Everything, sir!" I assured him. I was glad I could tell the truth.

"Nothing went wrong?" he asked.

"Nothing at all," I answered. There was no use worrying him.

"I've been feeding your chickens," Dr. Hendrix said in his hearty voice. "They're a mean bunch of birds, though. I get more pecks than eggs!"

The professor stared at Dr. Hendrix for a minute. Then he sat bolt upright in bed, and said to me, "That was my mistake, boy!" He sounded excited. "Those chickens *were* mean! We'll do the experiment again next year, but we'll use something gentle. I know what we can use. The eggs of a dove!"

When we left the hospital, the nurse said our visit had done the professor a lot of good. "He seems easier in his mind," she said. "He'll mend faster now."

"Poor old Botti," Dr. Hendrix answered, shaking his head. "He used to be brilliant. But listen to him now—rambling on about chickens and doves."

I said nothing. The professor wouldn't have wanted me to defend him. On the way home we talked a lot about the TV show. Dr. Hendrix had left his meeting at the university for a while so that he could see it. He said it had been really exciting. But I wanted most to hear what Mom and Dad thought about it.

My only worry was about winning the trip. I wanted Dad to go with me. I hoped Mom wouldn't mind. It was too bad it was only for two people. There was no way we could afford to pay for Mom to go too. Not with Dad out of a job again now that summer was over. I'd been trying not to think about that all summer.

What a welcome they gave me! Hank and Steve had made these huge Whiz Quiz Kid banners. Betty had baked a cake. It was a funny shape and I wondered what it was meant to be. Luckily she told me before I asked. It was Northanger Abbey. It was chocolate and tasted better than it looked!

"How did you manage to get that last question right?" they all wanted to know.

"I'd have said *Pride and Prejudice*," Mom said.

"I thought of *Emma*," Betty said.

I hadn't a clue what they were talking about.

"It was a baseball question," I insisted. Then I showed them my *Guinness Book of World Records.*

Even Joey joined in the laughter.

When I had told them every last detail about the television show, Dad said that he had some news.

"The lumber mill is opening up again in Woodgrove," he said. "I have a job starting right after Labor Day."

I was pleased. But then I thought about the World Series tickets.

"Will they give you time off to go to the game?" I asked.

Dad shook his head. "Not likely, son. We've been talking about that. Roy wants to go with you."

"Roy!" I said. "But he doesn't like sports!"

Roy grinned. "I'm really into competi-

tion after that quiz show! And seeing
they don't have a hacky-sack world series, I'll have to settle for baseball!''

113

I looked around at everyone. I felt really happy. We had all become good friends. It was like being part of a team. Too bad it wasn't a baseball team!

MARGARET ANDERSON is the author of *The Journey of the Shadow Bairns, Searching for Shona,* and three highly praised time-slip fantasies. She has also written nature and science books for younger readers. She was born in Scotland, graduated from the University of Edinburgh with honors in genetics, and worked as a statistician and laboratory assistant before marrying Norman Anderson, a professor of entomology at Oregon State University. The Andersons have four children and live in Corvallis, Oregon.

More Mystery Capers from Knopf

Man from the Sky, AVI
The Mystery on Bleeker Street, WILLIAM H. HOOKS
Mystery of the Disappearing Dogs, BARBARA BRENNER
Mystery of the Plumed Serpent, BARBARA BRENNER
The Robot and Rebecca:
The Mystery of the Code-Carrying Kids, JANE YOLEN
The Robot and Rebecca and the Missing Owser, JANE YOLEN
The Case of the Weird Street Firebug, CAROL RUSSELL LAW
Who Stole The Wizard of Oz?, AVI

Capers are. . .
"That rare series of fast-reading, high motivational
books which should be among the 'basics' in our schools.
Students will grab these books off the shelves
in any classroom or library."

—M. JERRY WEISS,
Distinguished Service
Professor of Communications
Jersey City State College